DARK SUN, DRY RAIN

A Collection of African Stories

© **Sylvia Somerville**

ISBN: 978-1-988031-02-6

This is a collection of Short Stories about my unique and fantastic experiences travelling around Southern Africa.
In 1978 I experienced my first walking safari in southern Africa. It was amazing! The stunning scenery combined with the beautiful wildlife and cordial people brought me back to southern Africa every year from 1978 until 1990. I was mesmerized with the sounds and emotions of the wilderness.

Dark Sun, Dry Rain

© Sylvia Somerville 2017

Dark Sun, Dry Rain is Dedicated To:

Ray David Somerville

My loving and devoted husband for fifty-five wonderful years.
Ray Somerville 09/20/1935 -04/20/2016

Jim & Lori Somerville and family

My son, my joy and my life

Christine Elaine Somerville

My daughter, my heartbeat, my sunshine and my life

Simon Cowell

My best friend, always with me in sunshine and storms.
My inspiration, my rock and my strength.

Dr. Drew Girard
Lorenza Hicks & Laurel Waldick

Thanks for your compassion and understanding and
always taking the time to listen.

Mayor Jim Diodati

Your friendship, kindness, and compassion.

Pat & Guy Girgenti

Your understanding, friendship and sunshine smile.

Only the eyes tell the truth:
not the stories one hears!

Ichobey boy, yachiki ilolonkude
Zulu Proverb

Only the eyes tell the truth; not the stories one hears.
Ichobey boy, yachiki ilolonkude
Zulu Proverb

The lion and lioness lay secluded, in the thicket beneath two umbrella trees, in full bloom with fragrant white flowers. The lioness knowing her mate was mortally wounded by the poacher's bullet that had smashed into his side. She tried cleansing the wound by licking the blood away but she couldn't stop the bleeding. It poured from the large gaping hole in his side. She soothed his agony with kisses and snuggled close to keep him warm. It was imperative they remain silent and still. The poacher's voices still hung in the night air. They were very close. If they found their hiding place they would slaughtered both of them for their personal pleasure. Life of these beautiful lions meant nothing to these evil humans!

Finally the voices faded into silence. The wounded lion moaned in agony. The lioness and lion knew he would die soon. The dying lion spoke to his mate with soft rumblings telling her to leave him and head for the safety beside the river. She caressed him, kept him warm with her body and licked the tears from his eyes. With his final gasp of breath she lay down beside him and tears ran down her face. The lioness softly cried. She felt the loneliness and and wanted to stay beside him forever.

The bullet lodged in her left shoulder had started to fester and ooze blood. She did not have the strength to stand. The evening breezes were rustling the tall grasses, with the sad sounds of the lion's death. She snuggled close to her dead mate and lay her head upon him and cried. Her mournful lament echoed throughout the vastness of the bush. Many animals replied to share her sadness and offer her encouragement and condolences. In her heart she felt her mate speaking to her. His spirit told her to quickly leave and seek safety in the conservation area on the Ntsiri River.

The lioness heeded her mate's message knowing

the poachers would return with the daylight and search for her. With the blackness of night to conceal her movement she cautiously crept out into the veld sniffing the air, seeking the poachers' scent. The acrid stench of cigarettes and burning wood was very close, northwest of where she stood. The lioness began her journey southeast towards the Ntsiri River and safety.

She travelled many hours with the moonlight to direct her while the cold night winds assaulted her. She struggled to keep moving and felt the hot blood oozing from her wound. Several times she rested and licked away the foul tasting blood and infection so it would not drip onto the ground and leave a trail for the poachers to follow. She could go no further. Her body throbbed with agony so she searched for a safe place to rest. She discovered a small crevice near the base of the cliff hidden behind thorny brush. It was not very big but she managed to crawl inside. She felt it was a safe place to rest. Reliving the poachers' guns and the painful death of her mate kept sleep from her. She rose with agony and stiffness and knew she must keep going. The movement reopened the wound and the oozing blood began flowing again. The pain was a hot fire, deep in her shoulder and her left leg would no longer support her. Her mate's spirit was with her and he encouraged her to continue and not give up. Limping badly, on her left front leg, she moved on, heading southeast.

Sunrise found her too weak and dehydrated to continue. She was hungry but did not have the strength to hunt for food. She nibbled on red berries and quenched her thirst at a small rock spring. The water was crystal clear and cool giving her renewed energy. Soon the sun was blazing hot. The lioness knew she had to rest. She snuggled down in the bushes and rocks, away from the trail. Her shoulder and leg were throbbing with pain. The lioness lay down to sleep. She dreamt of the poachers and felt her heart break remembering the agonizing death of her mate. A sudden loud roar followed with bright flashes awakened her. She lay silent, peering through her the branches and tall grass, expecting to see the poachers with their guns. The sound rumbled again, just before the rain. She lay down again and went back to sleep. She would continue her journey after the rains.

Around noontime we reached our camp. It has been a long, difficult hike, over the mountain pass and foothills. My friends and the rangers settled down, for a nap before dinner. I also lay on my cot inside our tent and tried to sleep. But I was overtired. Sleep was not coming. I decided to wander the area close to our camp site and take photos. There was no way I could know a wounded lioness was nearby. If I had known I would never have left the safety of our campsite, especially alone.

I wandered the foothills along the Ntsiri River, for a couple of hours before I discovered a herd of elephant busy with their dust ablutions. I crept as close as I dare, to take photos. Their bodies blended with the red-rust edge of the weather worn cliff face, as they covered themselves with red sand. I'm amazed with the deep red colour of the soil. When it rains, the water running down the cliff side looks like blood.

Pleased the elephant had not seen or heard me, I headed back towards camp. An hour or so later, the forest opened into a clearing. Cautiously moving forward my eyes caught a movement, a brown splash of colour in the bushes, about five feet ahead of me. But the African heat haze of a November afternoon, often creates illusions, so I dismiss my fears. Further along, I'm feeling a bit uneasy. I'm sure I just saw a lashing tail but it was likely a small animal gathering food. For a second, I was almost certain amber eyes, were watching me, from the edge of the forest. Once again I dismiss the thought when birds fill the sky almost blocking out the waning sun.

While climbing the last hill taking me towards our camp I realize how tired I am. It's been a hard climb through the drapery of tangle-thorn in the oppressive heat and I decide to rest, in the shade of the fever tree. I lay on my back, with my hat tilted over my face and cross my legs. Large birds are circling slowly round and round playing hide and seek amongst the clouds. The aroma of food cooking on the open fire, and voices filled with laughter from our campsite, drift on the air and disturb the silence. I decid it's time to make my way down this last hill and return to camp.

I hesitate a few more minutes watching the birds and enjoying the feeling of absolute peace. I hear a sound very close to me, but see nothing and again dismiss it. Likely the wind rustling through the tall, dry grasses. I am about to get up, when a large, dark shadow covered me. Unfortunately, the source of shadow wasn't dark clouds! A very large, tawny coloured lioness was sniffing my shoes.

I'm terrified! My first instinct is to get up and run, but I know that's the wrong thing to do. I remember rangers saying they owed their escape from lions and other wild animals by laying still and pretending to be dead. They claim the beast will lose interest and walk away. Now as I lay on the grass, with a lioness trying to decide whether or not to eat me, I understand why in such situations the ranger wouldn't move. He can't! Cunning be damned! Fear freezes you to the spot!

The lioness was straddled over top of me now sniffing my slacks. With her huge paw she slapped me on the thigh. I notice blood on my tan slacks and I'm sure she's going to kill me. When the lioness reaches my face she roars! A terrifying, earth shaking screech, with the stench of her breath and bloody spittle splashing onto my face. The odour is unimaginably foul! I'm certain she's going to kill me and I hope the rangers find me before she tears me apart for food and leaves the leftovers for the buzzards and hyena.

The lioness growls and steps over me knocking my hat off and growls again, deep and throaty. I open my eyes to see her moving clumsily away. My relief is short lived. She lay down under the trees, about twenty feet from me. She lay half curled up on her side with her forelegs crossed like a domestic cat.

It feels like hours have passed since she lay down, under the fever tree but it's likely only been minutes! A short time later I'm sure she's sleeping so I attempt to quietly rise and head for camp. She hears me, raises her head and growls a warning. I'm sure in the history of this area there has never been two stranger companions laying beneath the fever trees. To this day I don't understand why she sniffed me and lay down beside me, rather than have me for lunch! Trying to think of a way to escape, is taking up all my thoughts and even now, as I tell you about it, I expect you won't believe it. But I can only tell you the way it happened. Why? Only Africa and the lioness know!

The lioness hasn't moved in what feels like a lifetime to me, but again is likely only minutes. I'm sure the lioness is sleeping so I start moving without standing up, a few feet at a time. Once the lioness opened her sad eyes growled weakly and went back to sleep. It seems I've been here for hours, moving a few feet at a time. Finally I've managed to put some distance between me and the sleeping lioness so I think it's safe to stand up and run down the hill to the camp. Although my escape is almost assured there is a sadness deep within the core of myself. I'm not sure why I feel this sadness for the lioness. Probably because she didn't harm me. She is a magnificent creature. I wonder why anyone would ever want to kill her.

Back at camp, I tell my friends and the rangers what happened on the hillside beside our camp. Fearing for our safety, in case there is a pride of lions nearby the rangers ask me to take them to where I left the lioness. They have shotguns and tranquillizer guns, just in case

As we approach the fever trees, the lioness hasn't moved. She's lying, on the same spot, half curled up in the shade, her forelegs folded as before. But she's laying very still. Even from the distance we can see the large, red splash on her shoulder and side where the bullet had struck. I feel deep sadness and grief for the death of my friend.

I believe she knew I was a friend and would never harm her. She had lain beside her mate as he took his last earthly breath and perhaps she didn't want to die alone. All she wanted was a friend beside her as she died. I think when she growled that last time and closed her eyes, she died with me beside her and not alone.

The Place of Seagulls

Umuzi Ulwandle Inyoni - Zulu

The Place of Seagulls
Umuzi Ulwandle Inyon -Zulu

This morning dawned, as others have, but then again, it didn't. Somehow, it was different.

Koffee Bay was shrouded, in a stormy morning darkness. I sensed a strange touch in the wind and the trees sighed in rhythm with the warm, tumble of the sea. Outside my shuttered window wild protea and aloe danced in the hot, damp winds. They felt the coming storm. Heavy dark grey clouds scrubbed the mountain tops pushing away the white clouds. Rain would soon come.

At Em-Tandai, a small settlement near Koffee Bay, on the Indian Ocean where I was staying time seemed to stand still. Everything did seem a bit different than last year. The sea was bluer, the sand whiter, the sun hotter, the seagulls friendlier and the pineapples sweeter.

Walking along this wild coast I watched the tide gather strength and with a tremendous yawn, heave itself upon the rocks jarring all traces of sleep from their soul. Gulls squawked a warning, of the approaching storm and somewhere, off in the distance, an elephant trumpeted an echoing response to the thunder. Deep in thought, I'd wandered further than ever before. Just before the storm arrived, I came upon an old lighthouse and decided to seek shelter, until the weather cleared.

The wind had quickly risen to gale force and I was blinded by the blowing sand. Struggling to stay on my feet I heard a shrill, whistle piercing through the storm and I saw the blurry outline of someone waving me towards them. When I reached the ancient, old man, he took my arm and led me up many, natural rock steps, to the lighthouse residence perched atop the cliff.

Once inside the old man offered me a steaming

cup of hot chocolate and warm biscuits. He introduced himself as the lighthouse keeper, Zimilele Umbani Unlogolozi. His Zulu name meant, Wild Lightning Keeper!. Sipping my drink, I looked around at my surroundings, introduced myself, and thanked him for rescuing me from the fury of the storm and offering me refuge. Zimilele was an old, weathered man. He'd been keeper of the lighthouse since time began. He was a reclusive agent of wind and storm and watcher, of the skies. Most importantly, he became my friend. No one, not even the elders of the nearby Zulu Village, knew where he came from. The witch doctor claimed two hundred years ago, he was brought to earth on a lightning bolt!

The years had chiselled wrinkles and scars into Zimi's face. His tightly frizzled hair was sprinkled with silver and a small, wooden cross hung around his neck. He wore a pair of green shorts and a grey-white tunic, which was gathered loosely around his wizened body by a handmade hemp rope. There was an ancient smell about him, like that of an old attic, but his brown eyes sparkled with tranquillity. He spoke softly, almost a whisper. As for his age, he told me we grow older with the acquisition of wisdom, not years and revealing compassion with love and respect for others and nature, made one mature. As for how many years he'd been on earth, he couldn't recall, but spoke of tribal wars, almost ninety years past. There was an inner peace about this solitary man.

While the storm raged outside, it was warm and cozy inside. The entire house was bright, and I assumed he must have a generator, because there was no power, here on this wild rocky cliff. All too soon the storm had moved on but threatening black, storm clouds were again, gathering on the horizon and I knew I'd best head home or I'd be trapped here for the night. I thanked Zimi for his hospitality and promised to visit again.

Being a lover of seagulls, Zimi and I were drawn into a splendid friendship that ignored the generations of time, between us. Zimi's best and only friend, was a seagull he named, Kwelanga Umoya, which meant, sunsets soul. He and the gull were rarely apart. He seemed to understand what the gull squawked and he spoke to it in Zulu. I was convinced the two did understand each other when one afternoon I listened to Zimi speak to the gull and point out to sea. The gull flew away and returned with two huge steenbass fish, which he dropped at Zimi's feet. That was our dinner!

A few days later, when I met Zimi along the beach, near the lighthouse, a gull flew towards me and perched upon my shoulder. Kwelange was atop Zimi's head, as he introduced me to Ukupha uthanda, which means gift of friendship! Words of thanks and amazement escaped me. Zimi and I exchanged smiles and sensed the unspoken gratitude for the wonderful gift.

Uthanda was my constant companion and at the nearby Newanguba trading station, where I picked up my mail and supplies, the few whites staying in the area, called me an eccentric Canadian who talks with birds and mountains. It didn't bother me, what others thought. I'd discovered a side of life, beauty and friendship never experienced before. Zimi also gave me a Zulu name, Yedwa ulu Andle Inyoni, which means lonely seagull, because I was often alone beside the sea.

During one of our many afternoon visits Zimi entrusted me with the story about how he befriended Kwelange, many years ago. Apparently one stormy morning while he was walking along the beach, he discovered a small boy about six years old, unconscious between some boulders. The wild sea had cast him ashore amongs t seaweed, driftwood and stranded starfish. He was likely the only survivor of a shipwreck! He carried the lad home and after weeks, of nursing the child's battered body and comforting his broken spirit, the boy recuperated. Zimi named him Ukuphuma, which means sunrise because he'd found him after an early morning storm.

Zimi and Ukuphuma grew close and developed a deep love for one another. The child looked up to Zimi and called him father. The days echoed with laughter, while they shared life and disappointment. Zimi taught the child all about the sea, the stars, love and friendship. Ukuphuma learned to experience the feelings of the gulls and the storms; the movement of the universe and the journeys of the sun. He drank the knowledge with a devouring hunger and Zimi said when the two of them walked along the shore, nature sang in their hearts.

But, what the storm casts ashore, it reclaims with tomorrow's tides. Several years later, during a twilight storm, Ukuphuma drowned trying to rescue a seagull, with a broken wing, being dragged out to sea by a rip tide.

For many days Zimi sat upon the rocks and cried until his eyes were dried of tears and his heart was bled, grieving for Ukumphuma. Then one evening, from out of a mauve sunset, it's wings aflame with colour, drifted a seagull. It flew directly to Zimi and perched upon his slumped shoulders. Squawking and crying, the gull told Zimi he'd come to fill the empty place in his heart, now that Ukuphuma had passed beyond a shadow's reach. Zimi named the gull sunsets soul.

Zimi was a man of acute instincts. He could feel a storm, long before it arrived and people claimed he could control the elements and harness the power of a thunderstorm. He of course ,was not able to do this but, admittedly he was a bit strange at times. His lifestyle and habits were unique. He only drank the clear, blue dewdrops from an early morning spider's web and juice from the aloe plants growing wild in the area. . His only nourishment was an elixir of guava jelly mixed with pits, from choice fruits and vegetables. Naturally, people swore he'd mastered the art of ageing and some actually believed the witch doctors fable, that Zimi had come to earth aboard a lightning bolt.

His hobby was extremely strange and bizarre! He bottled the scent of thunderstorms! Whenever a storm gathered ominously over the ocean he'd launch his tiny, wooden dingy and row out on the wild sea, like a frail matchstick into the eye of the storm. He had attached a series of home made lightning rods, that he claimed, would systematically draw the raw charges of electricity from a storm, into the bottles attached at the bottom of each rod.

There was something, about the storms that broke at twilight that strangely affected Zimi He'd become very quiet and his eyes grew dark and serious. Sometimes he appeared to be in extreme pain, but he never uttered a word. Perhaps it was because a twilight storm had taken Ukuphuma's life.

Tribesmen would always gather on the cliffs, above the beach, to see him off, like morbid drivers slowing down at the scene of an accident. The storms were an obsession, with Zimi. Almost like a lifeline or rejuvenation! It was a true renaissance, for the old man, his intimate relationship, with an electrical storm!

Zimi knew Koffee bay in depth. He spent his lifetime with her, alone with Kewlange, when no one else saw her. This is how we became close friends, because I also enjoyed being alone at the shore, to experience the emotions of the sand, the sea, the gulls and straw-like flowers that carpeted the beach. Often, he was the only person alive, in the bay and long into the mid morning hours I'd watch him, from where I sat atop the dunes.

Many days and weeks disappeared while I sat on his porch listening to his stories. He sat in a home made hemp rope chair, eyes closed, amongst the

warmth of lanterns listening to a late summer night's
 silence.   Occasionally he'd gaze up into the heavens
and hum an uncanny tune and the ancient clock in his old
house, which sat atop the white rock cliff, would gong,
every time he stopped humming.   There   was no
electricity in the area, and he did not have a generator,
as I had previously thought, but his house was always
brightly lit.   Inside   the   house I   experienced the
wondrous smells of summer, and felt spirits of the past.

Nautical maps and chart parchments were laying
everywhere on shelves and tables. Magazines dating back
to 1929 were piled in a corner and the same ancient
clock that chimed along with his humming, ticked, slow
and steady, serving as the heart. In a large room, off of
the kitchen, was his study and unusual library, with books
from another time. There also, on the shelves, row
upon row, sat the strange bottles with uncanny labels.
The   unique   moon glow of their cabalistic treasures,
could be released on inclement days, when the sun has
not been seen for weeks and the rain is falling in torrent.

The root cellar resembled a wine cellar, only
replacing the vintage wines was a collection of a most

bizarre nature. The golden tranquillity of the calm before the storm.   The perilous twilight of April 14th, 1912. The stardust from Halley's comet, 1682 and in the far corner, stood his firefly net. The glow of the fireflies were the light and eyes of the house.

Zimi spoke in poetry and many nights disappeared, into the dawn while I sat, entranced by his stories of history seldom seen or   heard.. Not   of legendary conquerors or nations at war, but a history of the forces of Nature. Weather patterns, tidal movements, the journey of the sun, earth and moon and above all, the thunderstorm. Together we'd sit out on the porch, breathing the night, as did the house creaking like an aged, slumbering person.   Always Kwelange   and Uthanda were perched nearby chattering to us, when we fall silent. The panoramic view of the bay and crashing surf below,   allowed us an excellent vista as we'd watch   the storms   bank and roll in along   the sky bordered with stars, cool midnight air and the moon.

I saw in the old man's eyes things I'd   never grasped before.   Zimi was like a computer with a hard drive full of love, compassion and understanding. He was happiest when recreating the spirit of a bygone era with his stories and telling of his sorrow for today's people, who are afraid to openly care for one another. He commented about the changes in the bay over the years. The trees the eroding shoreline, the colour of the rocks, the sand and always he returned to the storms. No longer were they as intense, as in the past. Perhaps he said, the storms are growing old and weary, just like me. Each storm had a name and it would return annually. Every sunset gives birth to a new twilight and storms born at this time, and out of the west, are the most violent, he'd claim. The calm before the storm, the one magical moment when earths' forces are at ebb, was the time for gathering stamina and strength. Today I recall this remark and apply it in my daily life, always trying to summon my strength and courage before facing a difficult situation.

Zimi would say the difference between a fresh water storm and a salt water storm is the colour of the lightning. Lightning originating in the northern hemisphere may be silver-blue or white. A salt water storm born in the south, will have yellow-gold or moon-tan coloured lightning. Water density and temperature differentials are the artists. He expounded on the moon's undying thirst, for the bodies of water on earth, nightly casting its haunting caress, in hopes of an intimate, chance encounter. On and on Zimi enlightened me in the secrets of the universe, unfolding tale after tale on those nights spent, with this mysterious, but delightful old man.

The air felt like rain, but there were no clouds in the sky. From the west came the first rumblings far off, but moving fast. The old house shuddered. The bottles clanked nervously together, knocking several to the floor and I sensed this would be an unusually violent storm. We watched as it came rolling in over the bay. The sky grew heavy and the air was still. The house emitted a sigh like that of an autumn breeze and the old man became solemn and smiled, then looked away. The sky was now black. My eyes filled with tears and my heart bled because, I knew my time was up. This would be the last time I'd ever see this old man. The quiet talks in the dark, silenced forever. In that moment, after all this time, I only now began to realize who this ancient man actually was.   Zimi gave me a warm hug and smiled.   He had   never hugged me before and this confirmed   my feelings were correct.   He knew we'd never share conversation and laughter again.

The storm broke at twilight.   A strange feeling came over me, like when you're   abandoned, on the seashore by a close friend who has gone too far out, and you wonder if he'll return. Funny on that final evening,   no tribesmen   gathered on the cliffs.   I stood alone, Uthanda perched upon my shoulder and watched Zimi, with Kwelange settled on the bow disappear into the storm mists. He would never return.

A warm, early morning rain marked the end of summer.   Walking along the beach the old house looked like it hadn't slept either. The sea was moving quietly. Kwelange drifted out of the misty rain and perched atop my shoulder beside Uthanda, as I sat amongst the rocks, wondering and full of deep sorrow. Kwelange chattered away and I was shocked to realize I sensed his message.   He told me Zimi was at peace.   I was never to see the old man again or ever know for sure what became of   him.   He who had taught me all about friendship, life, beauty, wisdom and the movements of the universe. But, one day a year late, I thought I recognized him feeding the seagulls, beside the Niagara River. But,you know my imagination....

The skies shout of autumn with the strained, resilient death of another summer. February shadows run coldly out to meet the sea, as I walk along the crumbling high tide line of a sandy, desolate shore. An ancient house sits alone, dark and empty, like an old abandoned friend. Kwelange and Uthanda sit beside me on the porch chattering. My thoughts escape, into the silence and my heart is heavy with sadness knowing soon I must fly home and leave the two gulls alone. My heart feels it's more than I can bear having also lost Zimi, to the sea. Kwelange and Uthanda squawked together and somehow I knew they understood I had to leave.

As night falls I raise my eyes to the starry sky and say a prayer for Zimi who shared those warm and interesting evenings and filled my heart with the secrets of the universe. Returning to my rondavel Kwelange and Uthanda peck my cheek lightly and chatter. I kiss their beak and tell them I'll be back. Then closing my eyes sleep puts an end to what had been a summer like none other before or since.

Some nights I lay awake and wonder about the old man and my seagull friends. I hear the rumble of distant thunder and then I know. Seagulls gather and eat bread from my hand, along the Niagara River and I know in my heart, they're friends of Kwelange and Uthanda. My heart longs to return to Koffee Bay where I know they'll always   be waiting. Regardless, in my heart, every day, we share nature's gifts together Kwelange, Uthanda, Zimi and I.

You may get up before dawn,
but destiny gets up before you!

Urazinduka ntutanga rwuba
Zulu Proverb

*"You may get up before dawn,
but destiny gets up before you!"*
Urazinduka ntutanga rwuba
Zulu Proverb

A cold, autumn gale chills me, as I watch the fast moving clouds smother the last remnants of a dying sun. A lone gull dips and swirls, struggling against the high winds. Trees creak and groan, as they bend to let the winds pass, and waves crash spraying the rocky shore. At this moment, my solitude is priceless. Were anyone to approach me, ever so quietly, they would realize this old nature lover had slipped away midst seagull cries. Lost in reverie.

Memories had transported me back to Africa. I was no longer reclined in a chaise lounge, on my garden deck overlooking the Niagara River. Instead, I was sitting on a canvas cot, in a mud hut , near the Sabi River in Southern Africa. Many umbrella thorn trees, in full bloom, with fragrant, creamy white snowball shaped flowers, shaded my hut from the searing African sun. Water rushing over rocks, in a nearby river created a soothing chorus enhancing the sweet music of various songbirds. My camera equipment was packed and all was in readiness for a day secluded in a hide the Zulu ranger, UmSebe had erected for me. This area was renowned for photographing one of my favourite animals, elephant!

The dried water buffalo skin, serving as a door opened. UmSebe told me the hide was ready and he would take me there. It was built within the riverside brush, beneath a yellow barked Acacia tree, which offered shade and concealment. Here,I could safely photograph whatever wildlife decided to come to drink at the river. This was the dry season and many smaller rivers and pans had dried u, therefore, the animals would come here where there was still plenty of water.

When everything was organized inside the hide UmSebe and I went outside so he could instruct me, on how to approach elephant and other wildlife, on foot, should they choose to stop by today. He gave me a survival lesson. The do's and do nots, to stay alive and in possession of all my limbs!

UmSebe carried a cloth filled with ash from the campfire and swung it above his head, releasing the ash dust into the breeze. If the ash dust blows into our face, which it did, it was safe to continue. But, if the ash dust blew forward, it would carry our scent, to the nearby animals and put us in danger. He signalled me to follow and move exactly as he did. We crept along the rocks, in a low, crouch position, until we were in the open area beyond the pan.

"Never make a sound! Never, never run, no matter how frightened you are!" instructed UmSebe. "If you run the animal will chase and outrun you and attack! In the worst possible scenario play dead!. The wind is very changeable so check it's direction often. If animals pick up your scent, you will be in great danger!"

The sun was rising so we crept back to the hide for shelter and seclusion. Once the animals arrived it would be too dangerous to leave therefore, UmSebe had to return to our camp to fetch the water and food containers. Before leaving he assured me I was safe, "Stay in the hide and be very quiet." he said. "I'll return very shortly and when the animals come to drink, and if it is safe to do so, I will take you closer, to photograph them."

The first moments after he left I was feeling a bit anxious knowing I was all alone, without any protection. My imagination started working overtime.,

After what felt like hours of silence an elephant appeared at the edge of the tree line. Slowly she came closer to the pan. She stopped a few metres from my feeble hide. Only my eyes moved admiring her beauty. Following close behind was the rest of the herd. I watched in amazement, as one was eating grass near the edge of the pan. She would grasp the grass with her trunk and give a forward kick, slicing through it with her toenails. She popped the grass into her mouth and chewed. Shortly another herd of elephant appeared out of the morning heat haze and came to drink. They stood around the pan, like people in a park, murmuring, leaning on each other and watching their children play, in the water.

Without warning gusty winds came rushing in from behind the hide shaking the upper support branches, knocking a few down. The largest elephant turned and within seconds stood in front of me, trumpeting and kicking up sand and water. She shook her head and looked down searching for me, the intruder! I'm certain my heart stopped! I sat dead still, afraid to breathe, for fear she'd hear me! She was enormous and upset! For what felt like an eternity, but in reality was mere seconds, we stared at each other. I'm sure she could smell my fear! She trumpeted again and screamed! A deafening screech! I felt the heat of her breath, as her trunk brought down a shower of twigs and leaves, from the roof of the hide. There was a rapid exit path behind me for emergencies. I could quickly hop over the rocks, where it would be more difficult for the elephant, slowing down her attack. I contemplated using this exit, but fear kept me frozen to the spot!

The elephant not seeing me or finding the source of the unusual scent, calmed and moved away, leading her family back into the bush. Their thickly padded feet, made very little sound, as they left. UmSebe had warned me, never be over confident because an elephant could change its mind in an instant and charge! I sat still and silent. When the last of the herd disappeared, into the bush, my heart started beating again. Soon, the fear subsided and I relaxed.

Sitting alone in an observation shelter is a unique experience. I acquired bush eyes and ears. Waiting for the elephant to return, I had ample time to think. How did I end up in Africa. Well, let me start at the beginning. I was a volunteer, teaching creative writing at a junior School. About six months earlier, a teacher at the school had a visit from her Aunt, who lived in South Africa. The teacher knew I thoroughly enjoyed meeting and speaking with people and introduced us, and I showed her around the Niagara area. Together we enjoyed the attractions and became friends. Before returning home, she invited me to visit her in South Africa. So here I am!

A twig cracked and I thought I heard a child laughing. It brought me out of my thoughts and back to the hide. Several monkeys had come to the pan to drink. Their chattering resembled a giggling child. On the opposite side of the water, I saw the tall, sun bronzed grass moving and huge brown eyes peeked through the grass. Shortly several beautiful springbok appeared and wandered past the monkeys into the shallows. Soon they were frolicking and playing with the monkeys. Impala arrived, in a golden herd, their ears twitching. Soon the elephant returned. It was a heavenly day. The pan was filled with elephant, buck of many kinds, monkeys and a pair of rhino. Then, as if to complete the picture, giraffe slowly drifted out of the haze of sand heat and joined the others in the water. It seemed to me, all the wild life had decided to spend a morning, at the water, playing, washing, drinking and sunning themselves.

Overcome with excitement, I picked up my camera and ash bag. Slowly and quietly I crept out of the hide. Spinning the ash dust above me, it showed the wind was blowing towards me. I moved in the manner UmSebe had instructed, slowly, slightly bent and stepping as lightly as possible. I prayed the wind wouldn't change. As I moved closer, a rhino snorted and blew hot air in my direction. I stopped momentarily frozen to the spot. He glared at me and snorted again, this time twitching his ears. I think my heart stopped. I'm certain I didn't breathe for a few minutes. I began to think perhaps this wasn't a good idea. Maybe I should have waited for UmSebe. Too late! Apparently thinking I was a tree or something, he lost interest in me. My confidence returned.

Moving closer, a springbok turned and looked in my direction and I'm sure she smiled. Within the space of a few moments, I was in the middle of all that splendour. I was within touching distance of elephant, giraffe, rhino and yes, lions and cheetah. It's difficult to explain the exhilaration, with mere words. My long, solitary waits in the African heat had been rewarded. Although I can't begin to explain, I felt I had come home. My heart was overflowing with love and compassion for all these beautiful creatures. These extraordinary wild animals had accepted my presence and allowed me, the intruder, to wander amongst them. A lion looked in my direction and yawned, almost bored and obviously not worried or alarmed. It's as if they all knew I would never harm them. I'm sure they knew I was a friend.

As I relate this marvellous experience to you, my readers, I can only add that goose bumps appear on my arms and my eyes fill with tears, recalling the beauty, the splendour, the peace and tranquillity of Africa. Forever my footsteps will echo in her mountains, my eyes will laugh in her dark sun and dry rain and my ears will capture the melody of her surf and the songs of her jungle. My memory will always enjoy the wild tranquil solitude of Africa.

A cormorant calls in sleep
far up river
where night casts off her shadows
The Knysna flats beckon to incoming tides
Crying gulls drift in
Too early yet for prawn diggers

The sun
drowsy from sleep
pauses on the horizon
While gulls announce the dawn
Somewhere an elephant yawns

Peace awaits the soul
Beyond a shadows reach
Drifting under a dark sun
Drenched by dry rain
and soothed by the whisper of a star

The wind became erratic and I knew it was time to return to the safety of the hide. Before ducking under the security of branches, I stood for a long moment, admiring the spectacular vista before me. What have I done, I thought, to deserve this glory? It was more amazing than anything I could ever have imagined. I only hope to share this wondrous experience with mere words. It's an unspeakable wonder, I wish everyone could enjoy.

Inside the hide, sat UmSebe. He was smiling. Without being aware, he had returned to the hide. Although I thought I was alone, he was there, out of sight, but there all the time. He told me I had the soul of Africa in my heart. He never thought I would have the nerve, to approach Africa's wild and unpredictable animals completely on my own, unarmed! Also, he was surprised when the rhino, obviously caught my scent and yet did not charge. He said he had seen this only a few times

Perhaps UmSebe was being polite, when he told me the animals accepted me. They know my heart is with them.

Night comes quickly in Africa! So suddenly, it seems a dark curtain just falls and blocks out everything! This entire area will soon be covered, with the night time blackness that is indescribable, so we pack up and head back to my hut. Tomorrow we are heading north, by jeep, hoping to arrive at a private game reserve before nightfall.

The Place of Rest

Eku Pumuleni - Zulu

The Place of Rest
Eku Pumuleni - Zulu

While listening to the stars beneath a bush veld night, or hidden in tall sun bronzed elephant grass, we experience the wilderness bellowing with silence! This is the real Africa, but only a small fragment of the diversity, the magnificence and the varying degrees of echoing laments that will remain etched upon the heart and soul forever.

We feel a rare sensation drifting on the pale twilight enhancing our emotions that escape capture, with the rough net of words. Filtering shadows of dawn caress the tree tops, as the burnt orange sprinkled with green forests stretch deep below us. The scene is beyond definition as it blends into the brown scrub melting into the horizon. We enjoy this peaceful solitude, feeling the illusion of being suspended between heaven and earth.

The eastern sky suddenly explodes with crimsoned variances of burgundy and golden hues mingled with twinkling stars, as they begin to fade. A flock of Egyptian geese fly over the twilight water and alight, chattering, on a sandbar. Somewhere an elephant screams announcing the dawn. We sip our coffee while wisps of steam spiral upwards and others in the group crawl out of their sleeping bags to join us beside the campfire. In overhead branches monkeys screech a greeting to the new day. Vultures soar amongst the bizarre shaped clouds patrolling their domain, until the sighting of a carcass draws them back to the ground. We discuss our day's journey to a private game reserve on the border between South Africa and Mozambique. Our meagre supplies are loaded into the jeep and we head out before sun completely rises.

For hours we follow the Mkuze River, as it snakes through the LeBombo Mountains. Not far from here is the summit known to the Zulu as Tsheni, which means "the place of the small stone." As we drive through scrub, thorns and rocky outcrops we experience a strange sensation, hard to explain. It feels like something or someone is watching us. Hopefully we aren't being stalked by a pride of lions! Driving out of the heavy forest into a clearing we are greeted by tall, dead trees clinging to the cliff side, beside a waterfall. The cascading water looks like blood, as it mixes with the red soil of Africa. The trees are gnarled and twisted, giving a ghostly, haunted atmosphere.

We ponder the Zulu legend about this mountain. Perhaps this strange feeling means the mountain is haunted! Somewhere, high on this mountain scarred by deep gorges, heavy undergrowth, vines, thorns and strange trees is a taboo cave called Emakosini, the Zulu's sacred burial ground. The Zulu tribal chiefs are buried here along with their treasures and personal belonging's which are wrapped in a black bull skin. The trees and bushes and even rocks have unusual shapes which look like deformed animals. Often unearthly sounds echo throughout the gorge. Probably just the wind....or is it? We've been told Zulu spirits haunt this mountain. People claim to have seen strange flickering lights and trees that flame with fire but never burn. Perhaps the strange, unearthly sounds we hear are the Zulu ghosts! We stand silent, touching the souls of yesterday and wondering about the mysteries, waiting in our tomorrow.

It would be a fantastic adventure to meet a Zulu witch doctor, up close and personal and perhaps go into her cave. But, unfortunately we don't have time to search for the Zulu taboo cave o r resident witch doctor. We must be on our way if we hope to reach the game reserve before dark But, I make a promise to myself to return here and search for the cave and perhaps find a witch doctor willing to allow me access to the secret domain, where ever it may be.

Leaving the mountains, basking in an umbrella of dusty red sparks, the last remnants of a dying sunrise, we drive over the harsh, brown veld, scarred and cracked, from the long, dry winter. Several acres of ugly black ash and naked, skeleton trees, are the remnants of a recent fire. But, from every tragedy there springs beauty. Amongst this desolation, tiny purple and vibrant orange flowers peak up through the charred earth, creeping over the tangle of dead branches and grey ash.

Further along, the deep rutted clay trail, we have

been driving on, becomes a whole lot worse. Wild, black pigs wander along the trail, squealing, in their endless search for food. Stray cattle bleat a sad, melancholy prayer, as they scrounge the parched grassland, in hopes of finding nourishment. Zulu women and tiny children, their heads laden with large bundles of sticks, make their way toward the village of thatch roofed, mud huts, silhouetted on the horizon, clinging to the horseshoe ring of hills. In most African tribes, the women do all the work because the men are too busy being big, strong and brave!

For what seems an eternity, we make our way through the Lebombo Mountain's dense, tropical bush and trees covered with dripping moss and fungus. There is nothing here to remind us of reality or signs of civilization. No trading posts, no stores, schools or mission stations, only remote settlements of huts and natives sitting beside the mud game trail we are following, offering their wood carvings and beadwork for sale, to any who may venture this way.

Hours later, we drive through a high valley of

cold drizzle and fog. Beside the trail, we notice two small Zulu boys, shivering under their tattered blanket. As we approach, a thin, black arm darts out from its cover and frantically waves a pineapple! We stop.

Scampering over to our jeep, one lad said, "Please Englishman luscious fruit, yes?"

"A ngi gondi" I reply, with my terrible attempt at the Zulu language.

The other lad held up a pineapple and said, "Welcome chief. Luscious fruit, yes?"

Realizing they are selling the pineapples, I give the nearest lad a five Rand note.

He squealed, as they dumped twelve pineapples into our jeep. "Thank you. We see you chief."

Together they ran up the muddy hillside and into the bush, waving their blanket above them. It was several minutes before their delightful laughter faded away. Their joyous spirit remains in my memories, still!

The sun climbed to high noon, as we made our way through the mountain's rock formations unnerving sounds and ancient trees, dripping with moss and gauzy fungus. We feel years removed from civilization, within the splendour of this wilderness: the raw, natural elements from which today was fashioned.

Approaching Toorkip summit, known as "bewitched peak" to the Zulu, we worry about descending, this dangerously steep pass, as it cuts through the mountains, winding its way, into the remote settlement of Ubombo. Zulu legend claims this unusually steep and twisting pass was created, by an ancient witch. Apparently, one night the witch became baffled, trying to cross this mountain range. In her anger, she used her magic to violently split the rocks. Cautiously, we creep down, into the valley, far below. Many places along the way, one ranger had to get out of the jeep and direct the driver, over areas that actually ran behind a waterfall!

Near the centre of Ubomobo which consists of a café, trading post, post office and a few mud huts, we stop for lunch. At the café we enjoyed a hot bowl of meale-meale and a cold drink. We were told the toilets, were behind the trading post, so we went to use them. Walking down a narrow path, through thick underbrush, we find a sign reading, "Toilets." A bit further along the narrow path forks and signs indicate, "Dames" and "Men." Both paths led to individual thickets, complete with huge, buzzing red flies and an overwhelming stench. We decide to wait!

On the road again! We slowly and carefully make our way down the western slopes of the Lebombo range. The Pongola River carves its passage through the cliffs, towering for ninety metres, on each side. The vertical walls are studded, with green bushes, that somehow have found a foothold, on the rock ledges. Cacti, euphorbia and leafy bulbs droop overhead.

Needing a break, we park our jeep at the Golela trading post and trek, into the gorge, hoping to get some fantastic photos. Several chattering monkeys followed us, swinging along on vines in the overhead trees. Wandering along a dry riverbed is a bit easier, than struggling through the tickets and undergrowth. The November sun brought trickles of sweat, as we climbed over scattered rocks and fallen trees. The monkeys were ahead of us, overturning rocks, searching for a snack of scorpions or other insects. Rock dassies crept shyly along cordyla branche heavily shaded with g listening leaves, which they plucked, in passing. Dense bushes peeked out through rock crevices and over these, isolated tamarisks leaned into the gorge.

Sheltered, by an overhanging ledge, we discovered several rock pools, edged with lush grass and shaded by wild fig trees. We rested briefly. On the return trek to Golela, we stopped for a refreshing splash, in the Pongolo River, but our presence caused the many crocodiles, basking on the sandbars, to slide into the water. When a nearby log, floating down river crawled up onto the bank, very close to us, and transformed into a croc, we decided we'd rested enough!

A few hours beyond the secluded village of Ingwavuma, we photographed a spectacular vista of Zulu land, to the east and Swaziland, to the west! Continuing along this game trail, it became necessary for UmSebe to walk in front of the jeep, to keep us on the deeply rutted trail and direct us around trees. Thankfully UmSebe stopped us, before we drove over a hidden cliff, into the valley, far below. The game trail finally died! Progress and anyone lacking respect, for natures beauty, would never mar or destroy this intense solitude. They would never survive the journey!

Hot, tired and thoroughly exhausted, we all climb out of the jeep to stretch and decide which direction to go. The game trail ended at the cliff side and there was no indication, of which way to go. We were in deep forest which seemed to close in, like walls, all around us. We are certain this is not the trail into the private game reserve, but rather a trail into nowhere! Lying on the soft grass, to relax, I bumped my head, on a long board. Wow! It is the sign pointing to the game reserve.

So what direction would the arrow point to if it was upright? We decide to go northward. There's no trail to follow, so we make our own trail driving through thick brush tall elephant grass and twisting around trees. The forest is so dense in places we are driving through a tunnel of greenery and mysterious shadows.

The banks of the Usutu River are thick, with wild bala palm trees, known as the 'alcoholic palm' to the natives because the sap is a bit bitter but a refreshing drink. When the sap is fermented it becomes a powerful alcoholic drink! Throughout history, the natives have enjoyed this sap. They cut a groove into the bark of the tree and affix a long, narrow leaf, into the groove. The leaf acts as a spout, as the sap drips onto the leaf and into a calabash, a hollowed out gourd, used as a container, tied to the trunk. Result, free booze and powerful!

Fortunately we guessed right about the direction. Ahead and to the left, a flock of ducks rises up, from a nearby vlei, announcing our arrival as we drive through an overgrown entrance marked by two stone pillars. Here on the outer fringe of nowhere we feel the unique security of natures tranquillity. It doesn't matter that Marxist Mozambique lies just across the Usutu River! Thoughts about the closeness of Mozambique fades, soon after we arrive. The rangers carry sidearms, as well as other weapons and the huts are boxed in, and covered with thick steel mesh, so the grenades will bounce off, hopefully. But this area is so peaceful our thoughts dismiss any danger or terror.

Relaxing around the campfire, after a delicious meal of braised impala, meale porridge and strong coffee, darkness falls. Twice as many stars appear in a sky, much closer than the one at home, in Canada. This intriguing day comes to an end as we snuggle into our sleeping bags, on the dried, elephant dung floor of our thatch roofed mud hut. We speak in soft whispers, while outside, in the blackness, nature roars! Shout and you will spoil the mood.

The silence is so dense it keeps us awake the first night. The brash sound of a hippo clearing his nostrils, startles us. The laughing ranger reassures us. He tells us the hippo might be right outside our window. A few nights ago seven hippo wandered around this hut. Thankful for our exhaustion, we can almost dismiss thoughts of hippo and close our eyes hoping we won't be a midnight snack.

Loud crashing noises and sharp chattering startled us awake. "Nothing to worry about," shouts the ranger" just a few hungry monkeys outside."

After breakfast we prepared for our first walking safari. We are told to wear hats and hiking boots. This morning we're searching for rhino! We climb into the jeep and head out into the rising sun. A short distance from camp, we pass a grove of fever trees. Itt seems the trees have captured the sun and are saving it for a rainy day!

As we drive pass Nyamithi Pan cormorants dive off a log swimming underwater in search of a fish breakfast. Flocks of geese fly by, on their way up the pan. All that movement, all that life, but we remain still. We're the strangers, the intruders in this wilderness.

The ranger parks the jeep beneath a huge Baobab tree. From here, we are going on a walking safari to find the rhino. Making our way through the six foot, tall, sun-bronzed elephant grass, we could hardly see the person in front of us. The only sound is the rustling grass and nature shouting! Suddenly, there was a loud snorting noise. We stood silent, at the ranger's instruction. It was obvious, something large was charging toward us. The only source of protection was the nearby fever trees, but the lowest branch was about five feet above the ground. The ranger scampered up, one of the trees, to try and see what was ahead.

"Climb a tree," he shouts to us, "he's charging! He's heading this way!"

Sure! Me, climb a tree! I hoped the rhino didn't enjoy blondes, because there was no way I'd make it up a tree! The four of us stood there looking at each other. No one made a move. Apparently the others also thought as I did! No way! We heard the rhino coming! The sound was reminiscent, of a freight train, in a corn field! The sound seemed to be lessening. Thank goodness!

"It's alright!" Shouts the ranger, as he climbs down from the tree, "he's turned and is going the other way!"

Unfortunately we didn't find any rhino to photograph. Except for the one close encounter there seemed to be no more around. We did get photos of giraffe, monkeys and zebra, so it wasn't a complete loss. On our trek returning to the jeep, we hiked through the drapery of tangle-thorn, on weary legs. The scent of potato plant mingled with wild gardenia hung heavy in the air. Before climbing down the last hill we were treated to an amazing sight. A full, red orb of the newly risen moon hovered in our path seemingly within reach! Quite suddenly the glowing circle grew paler and rose up from the horizon, like a balloon. Spectacular! There was nothing to be said. No one could ever describe this wonder!

Finally back in the jeep and heading for camp, the wind in our face and sunset in our eyes we dodge the whipping thorns as they zip past all the while, absorbing this fantastic wild.

"It'll feel strange to get back to the reality of the city," someone comments.

"This is reality," I answered. "The cities are unreal!"

A fantastic variety of birds have adopted this conservation area as their home, along with hippo, crocodile, buck and the leopards and lions that prey on them. For us this is paradise. Very, very difficult to reach, but Shangri-La usually is!

Nights pass quickly and the days linger in the jungle. After some brief preparation we once again climb into the jeep and set out. We drive through flat, sandy, tree covered karoo scattered with pans, which are hollow impressions in the ground that have filled with water from the heavy rains. Many rivers tunnel beneath the trees and for miles is so dense the sun seldom penetrates through the roof of leaves to the water. So although the sun is shining brightly the sun is dark! Wild bala fig trees and forest giants line the rive r banks and their branches meet overhead forming an arch over the river. The monkeys and baboons use these branches to cross the rivers safely.

Our guide is a bird expert and spots a wide variety of birds before we notice them. He tells us the Bou-bou birds sing duets and the Kingfisher can hover and fly backwards! The Black Heron fishes from beneath the umbrella canopy he makes with his wings. This reduces the suns reflection on the water, while he wiggles his yellow feet to attract his prey.

Apparently the black rhino usually spends time at the Usutu River, so the driver pushes his foot down and the jeep bucks and crashes through the undergrowth. Beside the driver sits a marksman, with his specially fitted rifle, carrying a large hypodermic needle filled with tranquillizer. We bounce over the wild terrain of dense bush, thorn trees, river beds, dongas, rocks, shale and sand. This, we're told is rhino country.

Suddenly, a massive, black rhino crashes out of the thicket , in front of us. Upon seeing us he darts back under cover and disappears. The jeep slams through the undergrowth and we duck, covering our face and eyes to protect them from the slashing thorn branches. Soon a gigantic black backside comes into view directly ahead, but disappears again into the brush.

The ranger, myself and a couple others follow the rhino tracks on foot through thick undergrowth and mud, while the smart ones remain beside the jeep. Now we realize why hiking boots or waders were recommended footwear, as the muddy swamp water sloshes inside our nikes. Slushing along a wallow we hear the reeds snapping. Something, probably the rhino is crashing towards us. We stand still and silent. The danger passes. Our camera shy rhino has lumbered off and it's much too dangerous to keep following him further into the dense thickets. So we head back to the jeep with muck, swamp water and twigs clinging to our clothes and sloshing in our shoes.

Back in the jeep, with windscreen down flat, we remove our mud caked shoes and brown, soggy socks. The ranger says something in Zulu to his marksman who joins in his laughter. We are now heading for Red Cliff where directly across the shallow Usutu River stretches Mozambique. At nigh, when the crocodiles sleep, the poachers cross the river and catch impala an inyala. Obviously, the poachers are the present problem, not terrorists. The Zulu guides toss stones at the sleepy crocs chasing them off the sand bar into the water. Perhaps one night the crocs will stay awake and poach the poachers.

Finally with the hot wind on our face and the sun set in our eyes, we dodge the thorns, as they whip past heading back to camp and the end of another intense day. Leaving the Zulu guides to set up camp and cook our supper a few o f us accompanied with an armed ranger go for a short walk.

We are treated to the sighting of a herd of water

buffalo feeding noisily along the swamp reed bed. Suddenly we see a flash of silken orange and a leopard slides momentarily into sight, just below the rocks where we stand. A water buffalo bellows followed by the lowing bleat of a calf lost in the bubbling song of a coucal's crescendo.

Warthogs are resting under the trees, while several kudu bulls, with immense horns move through the bush. Nearby a pair of steenbok keep close company, the buck is sleek and muscled and the doe hornless, her face glowing with a feminine sweetness. The aroma of buffalo dung lingered around the spoor where scores of hooves had passed, a few hours earlier. Crested guinea fowl are rasping themselves to sleep, as the night's wild lament, heralds the coming darkness.

Back at camp, there is much to absorb and share, at the end of each enthralling day, as we watch the embers dancing in the campfire it seems to epitomize the freedom of the wilds. There is still one thing to do. We haven't taken photos of dawn. We've seen sunsets. Spectacular sunsets but dawn must be amazing. The rangers encourage us to spend our last night, sleeping outside beside the river, to enjoy the dawn. We head to a narrow spit of land ringed by fever trees which catch the lights of the jeep. I was right! The trees do trap the sunlight! Tired but excited, we snuggle into our sleeping bags, set under the open sky, above the river. In the morning, we must leave this paradise. Something we'd almost forgotten. My heart has become one with the beauty and solitude of Africa.

The night winds sweep up over the pan, bringing rain clouds. But unfortunately it looks like it will hold off. Shame. With the treacherous road conditions a rain storm might trap us here forever.

The incredible jungle darkness surrounds us. It's almost tangible. We worry about hippos and crocodiles. What was that noise in the shallows? Of course it's only the wind brushing the water and shuffling through the vines. Night wears on bringing a crescent moon to brighten the sky. Something splashing at the waters edge freezes us in fright. No one moves. Needless to say we don't sleep much for fear of missing something or perhaps for fear of something not missing us.

Dawn! The morning sun peeks out from behind a bank of rain clouds. With the force of an explosion a pillar of fire shoots upwards, from the blazing orb, expanding into gauze strips of dusty rose hues bouncing between the clouds. A huge hippo strolls out of the water and heads towards me, as I sit atop my sleeping bag, photographing the dawn. "Stay still," shouts the ranger" he'll go right past you. You're not in his path, but if you move you'll startle him and he may charge!"

Fine for you, I'm thinking. I'm the one about to be trampled to death! I sit dead still. My heart is pounding so loud, I'm certain the noise will startle the hippo. But the ranger is right. The hippo strolls by a mere 10 feet from where I sit. It's a frightening experience but also spectacular! Closer to the water a mother hip po, with a baby on her back, watches me gravely. She wiggles her pink ears at me. Can you imagine being greeted in the morning by a hippo? Awesome!

The sun climbs, moving from the top of the trees, down their trunk to the ground. The game reserve has awakened. Two fish eagles rise up over the pan, to greet the new day screeching the wild cry of Africa A ten foot long log floating down river climbs onto the sandy bank and transforms itself into a crocodile. What a tremendous yawn. Wow! Impala approach the river to drink, nervous and always on the alert for whatever might reach up out of the water, or lunge out of the bush. Many, many birds fly upriver to areas where they usually congregate to eat their vegetarian breakfast. Sun bird, white-faced duck, king fishes, all fly past We're in the middle of all this splendour. This is their domain. We are the intruders.

The Zulu guide loads our camping gear, into the rover, while we remain beside the sandy river, absorbing the last few moments of Africa's tranquil solitude. The surging, sweeping process of life; the movement of worlds; the journey of the sun and the moon, become acutely vivid within. This wilderness paradise gives us a glimpse of eternity.

We return to our huts, aching backs, sore, red eyes and no one is speaking. The sun was fast approaching mid day when we leave the reserve, driving into the rain. For several hours we see no cars, but as we reach the city there seems to be too much. Too much traffic! Too many people! Too much unnatural noise!

But, there is consolation. We can always return, even if we can't stay there forever!

Give Thanks To God If You
Live Long Enough To Grow Old!

uWakiz'ubusore aba agize Imana

Give Thanks To God If You
Live Long Enough To Grow Old!
uWakiz'ubusore aba agize Imana - *Zulu Proverb*

The elephant is the true king of the beast, but the lion is the warlord.

Our days trek was very exhausting and difficult. Around mid day we rested beside a river bank, shaded by willow, bala palm and tambotic trees. Somewhere, nearby a hippo grunted! There's something special in the air today difficult to express. Is it the faint breeze touching the hig h tree crowns or perhaps the brown, green tinted infinity of woodlands and scrub that merges with the horizon. Maybe it's that constant illusion of feeling suspended between sky and earth, drifting free of today's uncertainties and tomorrow's sorrow.

We feel the depth of peace and solitude, laying here amongst the river bank sand on a blanket of wild flowers watching the graceful flight of a gull soaring majestically without conscious effort, unharnessed by such mundane limitations as gravity, or pain, in his no man's land of thermal currents. We have an intense desire to soar with him, into his unknown world of space and freedom, no longer bound to earth.

Without warning, our wandering thoughts are pulled back to reality by the sighting of a huge, lion's head with very full bronze and dark brown mane rising out of the low bush, about twenty feet from where we lay. The lion yawned, with deliberate arrogance and stretched his taunt, muscular body in one rippling movement, before lowering himself back, into his private hiding place, where our eyes could not follow.

In the distance we could hear the enchanting echoes of drumming coming from iBubesi's Village. As we drew closer we met umKlombe, one of the villagers on his way to the river to get water. "There's beer tonight," he said, grinning widely. Since he'd already sampled the beer, he was not his usual coherent self. The large amount of mnealie porridge we saw already cooked and the many drums of their home made beer, meant the party would go on all night. We continued on to our camp, a short distant from the Village.

By the time we headed back to the Village to join in the festivities it was dusk. We always marvel at the sunsets in Africa. Tonight the giant marula trees were silhouetted against a burnt orange and rusty yellow sunset. The euphorbia trees, with their long green stems, stood like sentries, on the horizon. The fading colours of the evening, a grunting hippo and the last song of the weaver birds broke the stillness before the croaking of the frogs. Suddenly darkness, the hollow thumping of native drums and the reflection of moonbeams on the river.

We'd almost reached the village when the air was suddenly shattered with the shrill trumpet blast of an angry elephant. Hurrying into the village to see what was wrong we saw a tall mopani at the edge of the trees explode with fire and black smoke. Then the burst of singing which meant the party had begun.

Another elephant screamed. The drummers seemed to lose their rhythm. We were still about a half mile from the camp but every sound travelled clearly on the still air. Even the pungent smell of native beer which they brewed in large vats on open fires drifted around us like fog.

Without warning a pillar of fire showered sparks into the trees, setting some dry leaves alight. Several elephant silhouetted as they passed across the blaze. We climbed a nearby anthill for a better look, and felt completely helpless. A trampled hut flamed. Terrified shouts and the trumpet sound of an angry elephant and deep throated roars shattered the silence.

One by one the huts crackled and burst into flames. Shouts, curses, and the agonized screeching of elephants silenced the drums. The burning village was bright as daylight. A large bull elephant took short, quick steps and dipped his trunk into every earthen pot on the ground.   Hot porridge scalded him!   Running and screaming the elephant destroyed another hut. The fire was so close it scorched his behind and his high pitched yell hurt our ears, as he trampled another hut.

Then he saw the grain bin, on a platform ten metres high. He began to rock the grain bin until the legs snapped and the bin fell with a roar, spilling pale yellow corn. Three cows curled their trunks and scooped the grain into their mouths. Their teeth crunched the corn as if it were toast.

Another bull elephant with long thick tusks moved beyond the blaze and found the vats of beer he inserted his trunk.   While drinking the beer with gusto a lot of it ran down his chest and legs. He seemed to be having a beer shower.   Soon, he began swaying becoming drunk from drinking so much beer. He carefully spread his legs, one by one, to balance himself.

Thick, black smoke covered the village hiding the natives as they ran towards the river to get away from the elephants and   for safety from the fires.

Blinded by the smoke the elephants bumped into each other, as they staggered around, not knowing which way to go, until the bull elephant led them to the water. Putting one foot in front of the other, very carefully, the large tusked elephant began weaving towards where we stood atop an anthill. . His eyes rolled and his head swung with each step. Twice he stopped and sighed with a loud exhale of air. His swaying body scraped against trees, and leaves fell like rain.

We saw the whites of his eyes, as he passed about two metres from where we stood. His legs were well spread trying to balance himself. Then his hip caught on a tree limb and he leaned against it at an acute angle. He burped with the juicy sound of a rising vundu. He arched his back and rocked to and fro, his skin sounding like sandpaper as he brushed against the tree bark. Suddenly his stomach squeaked, and rumbled loudly as the wind escaped and with a sullen report, the pressure was released.

Our eyes were streaming with tears and we shook with laughter. The bull elephant heard the unusual noise and looked in our direction. Satisfied we were part of the ant hill he closed his eyes, curled his lip in a sneer and filled the air with his bubbly snores.

UmKlombe appeared out of the bush looking confused. "I don't think the elephants hurt anyone" he laughed, "he's had a happy time. We'll find out in the morning and will deal with him then. But what about my beer! It's all gone!"

Ignore Pain And It Flies Away! Maybe

Dema Ikuna Kamagachin Kushumudi! Mhlawumbe
Zulu

Sunshine
is lost today
in sadness
memories
and dark clouds

Somewhere
the fog is lifting
Somewhere
there is happiness
Somewhere
Well
maybe not

Sunshine
is lost today
hidden in fog
hopelessness
and a broken heart

The lion is hungry
he sees
the shattered heart
The lioness is hungry
she also sees
the broken heart

But instead of a meal
to satisfy themselves
they walk away
Hoping the heart
will heal

But it can not
the wind
the sadness
life
Has scattered the pieces
some torn
beyond recognition

A discarded jigsaw puzzle
pieces lost in the wind
hidden under heaviness
destroyed by the tears

But still
the sun might find
the shattered heart
and it will heal
Maybe
maybe not

The Mountain is Collapsing!

Ku Dilike Intago
Zulu

The Mountain is Collapsing!
Ku Dilike Intago
Zulu

The window of my thatch roofed, mud hut offered an excellent view of the Usutu River. I noticed only the tree tops were touched with patches of green leaves. Everything else was a straw yellow, moontan and sand dust colour. Dark black water, from the gray rocks on the cliff side, sparkled in the sunlight as it dropped into a shallow rock pool. The trickling water ran along a sandy, dry river bed and dried quickly. It appeared to be like dry rain because it was wet when it left the rock pool above but dry when it reached the river bed.

This is the African dry season! The ground was parched and cracked. The air was dry and abrasive and the wind carried the taste of dust. Two acacia trees stood like giant umbrellas on either side of my mud hut giving me some shade from the searing sun.

During the month of October trees takes on a skeleton appearance, standing naked and sunburnt. The leaves and bushes twist and curl. Dry grass crackles and the ground is too hot to walk upon barefooted. But then the day finally comes when the acacia tree tops are covered in little green leaves. Every day more trees will begin to fill out with fresh, new buds. This is the first sign the rains are coming.

Around mid day I could feel the anticipation of the villagers watching and waiting for the forest to become a blanket of green. Wildlife drifted from one shady spot to another, their eyes and nostrils half closed, waiting for the cool of twilight to go in search of food.

Suddenly it seemed all the trees turned and looked up at the great flat clouds beginning to build on the horizon. Each day more and more clouds filled the sky, rolling and tumbling passed.. The clouds would change colour and shape with the sunset and sunrise each day.

Finally the breeze from the river joined the wind from the hills and every tree twisted and bent wildly, as the gales rushed in scattering twigs and sand into the air. Elephants trumpeted and shrieked. Monkeys screamed. The wind was bringing the rain! Clouds choked out the sunshine and for a moment, everything was silent. The air grew heavy as the sky darkened and lightning split open the clouds accompanied by claps of thunder. Doors and windows were quickly closed and latched. The villagers hurried to tie things down and store the firewood inside. Chickens and hens scattered seeking shelter.

The wind eased again and the hot damp silence sat beside me and waited. All the animals had taken shelter and the only sound was the coo coo of the spotted dove and the plaintive pipping of the hornbill. Occasionally a heavy drop of water smacked the ground. I felt as if heaven lay close to the earth and I sat between them.

Slanting streaks of yellow lightning swept across the valley and the thunder bloomed louder. The dried thatch roof of my hut shifted as the first rain drops fell washing away the dust. This was the sound the village had been waiting and praying for. The air cooled and the fragrance of moist earth filtered into my hut. I could almost feel new life growing up from the ground. I felt like singing and only now understood why the Zulu were so thankful for the gifts of nature.

The rain fell in torrent, pounding the ground. Nothing would stop it now. I lay down on my cot, a lantern on my night stand and closed my eyes listening to the drumming on the roof. Where moments ago the barren earth lay parched, a brown sheet of water rushed by spraying the mosquito netting of my open window, creating puddles on the mud and cow dung floor.

Within the hour the rain had moved into the hills. In the stillness of the valley soaking wet trees shook off rain drops falling with loud splatters onto the ground. I walked barefooted across the red, muddy ground jumping and hopping over puddles. Patches of blue sky appeared and sunlight glistened on the dripping bushes. The quenched earth absorbed the water causing steam to rise in a mist.

In the distance I heard a strange rumble and looked up. The noise grew louder and louder until I realized water was rushing somewhere on the cliff, above where I stood. Suddenly the mountainside erupted and a thunderous gush of dark brown water leapt over the edge carrying trees and rocks along with it. It rushed into the rock pool over flowing into a narrow gorge and filling the dry river bed. Where gray rocks and yellow grasses had stood, now muddy water churned.

Darkness fell. Distant thunder shook my hut as lightning slashed through the sky illuminating the distant mountains on the other side of the river. The rainy season had arrived. It rained for three months. Entandei was redecorated from pale colours to those of lush green and vibrant orange. Life changed with the rains. Everyone in the village felt rejuvenated.

Epilogue

We live in a global community today and everyone has a purpose, a place and are needed! We must respect and help each other and speak up and protect those who cannot speak for themselves.

Nature and all animals, domestic and wild are a part of us. We must protect them and take care of them. I have heard it said the wildlife is infringing on our communities but think about it, we have taken away their forests and wilderness and built cities and homes. The wildlife is often confused and they don't understand why the bushes where they enjoyed their wild berries are gone and strange structures now stand there. Show compassion and understanding and help relocate the beautiful wildlife instead of killing them.

Preserve our natural resources. If we don't the day will come when there is no fresh water to drink, no more trees to fertilize the ground and provide shade and protection from the elements. This world will become a wilderness of bleached boulders. A dead garden full of blowing straw and skeletons of blasted trees. We can not grow food in sand with no water. We can not exist without natural resources and our wildlife. Thank you.

Here are a few noteworthy captions:

I discovered these while researching a few things to be certain Dark Sun, Dry Rain was accurate. When I speak about the different trees, etc. Following is what you call different groups of wildlife. I found it interesting and hope you do as well.

A clan of hyena;   A leap of leopards;
A dazzle of zebras;   A memory of elephants;
A prickle of porcupine;   An armoury of aardvarks;
A pod or raft of hippo;   A crash of rhino;
A parliament of owls;   A whoop of gorillas;
A confusion of guinea fowl;   A convocation of eagles;
A business of mongoose;   A pride of lions;
A hedge of herons;   A coalition of cheetah;
A bask of crocodiles;   A flamboyance of flamingoes;
An obstinacy of buffalo;   A wake of vultures;
A gaggle of geese;   A pod of pelicans;
A tower of giraffe (when standing still);
A journey of giraffe (when moving)

About the Author, Sylvia Somerville

 Sylvia Somerville (Pine) was born and raised in Niagara Falls, Ontario, Canada and attended Maple Street School and N.F.C.V.I. She has been writing since a young child and had her first poem published in the Niagara Falls Review's Wit, Wonder, Wisdom column when she was seven years old. She studied and performed dance for 12 years and was an accomplished musician on the 'cello and piano and appeared in many musical productions.

Sylvia is a Board Member of the Niagara Arts Showcase, served as President of the Chippawa Business Association and the Willoughby Historical Society. She is an active member of the Greater Niagara General Hospital Ladies Auxillary and the Pilot Club of Niagara Falls. Author Somerville worked as a correspondent for the Niagara Falls Review before becoming owner/publisher of the Chippawa Times Newspaper. She believes volunteering is important and has worked on the Niagara Falls Canada Day Committee for 23 years. Sylvia also writes and illustrates Children's Books.

She enjoys wildlife, nature, long walks along the lakefront, hiking, cycling, photography, writing poetry, music and travel. Her love of wildlife, nature, people and sunsets will be obvious to all readers of "Dark Sun, Dry Rain" and all her creative works.

Other Book Titles by Author, Sylvia Somerville

Tribulum
Wind Echoes
Lost Behind The Wind Echoes
Sondela (Farewell)
Dark Sun, Dry Rain
Life Is A Jigsaw Puzzle

Children's Book Titles

Simon Lion Discovers Elephants Have Hair
Friends Are Like Rainbows
A King's Tale
Simon Lion's Adventure on the French River
Simon Lion's Niagara Falls Adventure
Simon Lion Discovers Secrets Behind Niagara Falls
Simon Lion Meets The Legendary Dragons Behind Niagara Falls
Simon Lion's Magical Adventure
Simon Lion's Raindrop Friends

www.ingramcontent.com/pod-product-compliance
Lightning Source LLC
Chambersburg PA
CBHW061524050726
47503CB00016B/2720